ERNST

Elisa Kleven

A PUFFIN UNICORN

PUFFIN UNICORN BOOKS
Published by the Penguin Group
Penguin Books USA Inc., 375 Hudson Street, New York, New York 10014, U.S.A.
Penguin Books Ltd, 27 Wrights Lane, London W8 5TZ, England
Penguin Books Australia Ltd, Ringwood, Victoria, Australia
Penguin Books Canada Ltd, 10 Alcorn Avenue, Toronto, Ontario, Canada M4V 3B2
Penguin Books (N.Z.) Ltd, 182-190 Wairau Road, Auckland 10, New Zealand
Penguin Books Ltd, Registered Offices: Harmondsworth, Middlesex, England

Library of Congress number 89-1634
ISBN 0-14-054944-7

Published in the United States by Dutton Children's Books,
a division of Penguin Books USA Inc.
Designer: Barbara Powderly
Printed in Hong Kong by South China Printing Co.
First Puffin Unicorn Edition 1993
1 3 5 7 9 10 8 6 4 2

ERNST is also available in hardcover
from Dutton Children's Books.

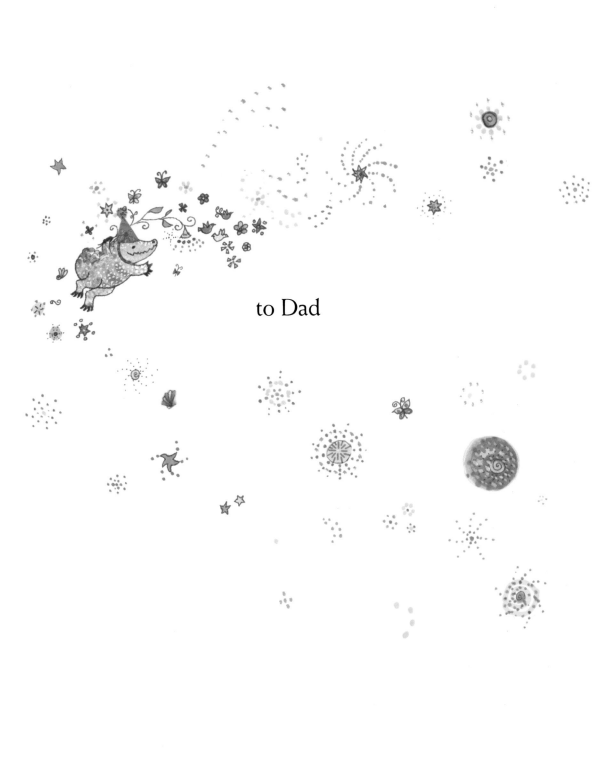

to Dad

Once upon a time, in a world full of light, trees, bugs, seashells, birds...

and night, there lived a young crocodile named
Ernst, who loved to think "What if?"

"What if sand were fudgy instead of sandy?" he'd think when he dug damp holes at the beach.

"What if everyone traveled in magic carts?" he'd think on the hot bike ride home.

"What if grandmas were young?" he'd
think when he sat on his grandmother's soft,
wrinkled lap.

"What if trees never dropped their leaves?" he'd think when he painted the tree outside his window.

"What if the honking school bus could
sing?" he wished one day as he trudged off to
meet it.

"What if the stars were big?" he asked his
mother that starry night as she scurried around
the kitchen.

"The stars *are* big," said his mother.

"How big?" asked Ernst.

"Big," said his mother, rolling out the crust for double fudge pie. "Big as worlds. Please get the chocolate and sugar from the pantry, sweetie."

"Mother," said Ernst, as he got the chocolate and sugar. "What if fudge were black-and-white striped, like a zebra?"

"Please call Father down for supper," his mother replied.

"Mother," said Ernst, when he'd called his father. "What if Father were called Pumpernickel instead of Father?"

"Wash up for supper now, Ernst," said his mother.

"Mother and Father," said Ernst at supper. "What if I were a little yellow bird who lived all alone on the moon?"

"If you were a bird like that, then it would be hard for you to eat your dessert," said his mother, handing Ernst a serving of jiggling green Jell-O.

"Mother," said Ernst, as he nibbled his Jell-O. "Why aren't we having double fudge pie for dessert tonight?"

"You know why," said his mother. "Now what if you finished dessert, brushed your teeth, and got into bed?"

"Mother," said Ernst as his mother tucked him in. "What if my birthday came every day?"

"Then it wouldn't be special," said his mother. "Now go to sleep, because tomorrow *is* your birthday."

"I know!" said Ernst, and shut his eyes and thought, w h a t

i f .

.   .

he got a spaceship for his birthday,
and blasted off, zooming deep into
the dark, sparkling sky, past zillions
of swirling stars, whirling suns,
comets . . .

past meteors, asteroids, galaxies, and moons, until he reached a faraway world...

where sand was fudgy, and
everyone traveled in magic carts...

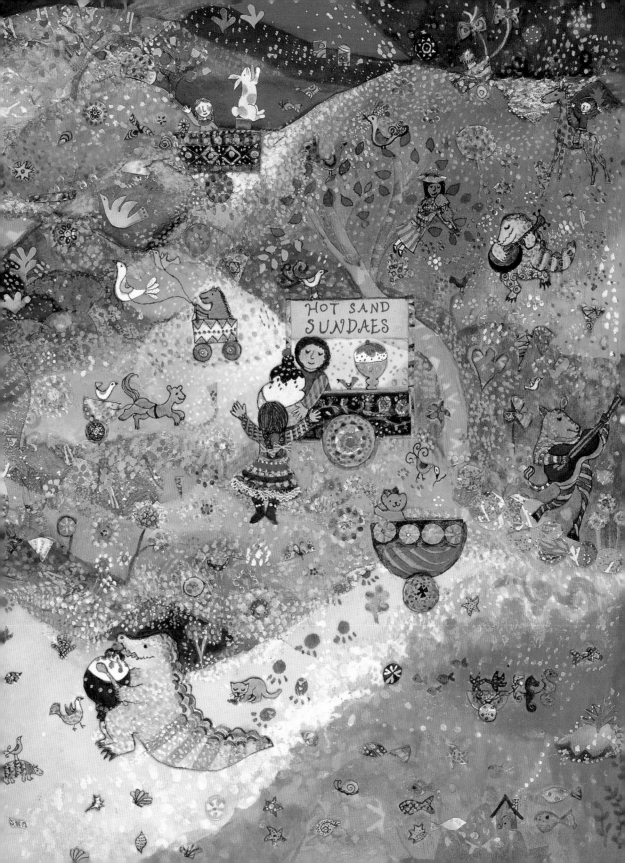

and grandmas were
smooth as ladybugs (and fit
in the palm of your hand),

and trees held on to their leaves
all winter, and the stars above
were no bigger than seashells...

and fudge looked like zebras,

and fathers were called bagels,

and mothers answered every question you asked them. It was a strange and beautiful world.

Back in Ernst's own world it was morning,
and Mother, Father, and Grandma were
waiting with presents and sparkling hats...

and instead of oatmeal for breakfast there was
double fudge pie,